Dolly Does Her Job by Susan Langlois

Copyright 2019 by Susan Langlois

Illustration and Cover Art by Daniela Frongia

Cover and interior layout and typography by Qamber Kids

For Dolly, and every animal waiting to be rescued.

For my sisters and my mom – Deidre, Sharon and Mary. Together first, and forever.
For Dee and John, who have changed countless furry lives through
rescue, foster, adoption and love.
For Ray, thank you for encouraging me to do 'my job'!

Love. It always protects, always trusts, always hopes, always perseveres. Love never fails.
1 Corinthians 13:7-8

This book belongs to:

_____

Dolly does her Job

WRITTEN BY
Susan Langlois

ILLUSTRATED BY
Daniela Frongia

"There's a dog in here!"
She scooped me up from the lonely hole
and combed out my hairy knots.
"Hello there, furry friend!
I'm Dee."

She took me home and made a comfy bed. I was happy to say goodbye to the lonely hole.

Day after day, Dee brushed my hair into a shiny, bouncy hairdo. "You are as pretty as a doll," she said.

"You're my Dolly." That's a nice name for me, I thought.

Soon I learned tricks like "come," "sit," and "stay."
I practiced and practiced for many weeks. My favorite
trick was "snuggle." Nobody had to teach me that.
I just knew.

DOG SCHOOL

One day, after I'd done all the tricks right, Dee exclaimed,
"You've done a GREAT job. Dolly!"
I loved doing my job.
"Tomorrow," Dee said, "you'll be working in a place
with lots of children."
Children?
"I'll be with you all day long," Dee added. "You'll do a great job."
I wasn't so sure about that.

The next day was the first day of school.
I never could have imagined a place like this. There were so many kids.
They were inside and outside, coming and going. Some had bags,
some had boxes. They were everywhere!
The kids stared and stared at me. I guess they never could have
imagined a working dog like me.

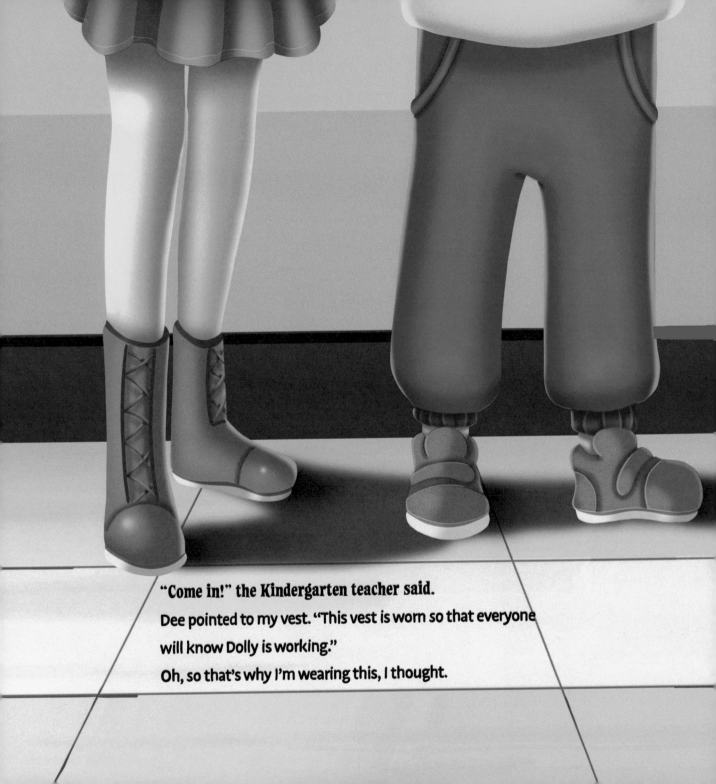

"Come in!" the Kindergarten teacher said.

Dee pointed to my vest. "This vest is worn so that everyone
will know Dolly is working."

Oh, so that's why I'm wearing this, I thought.

During reading class, the teacher told the kids to go and
read together, but a boy named Tony didn't want to.
So, I sat with him. Thump! Thump! Thump! A drum was
beating very fast inside his chest. It was time to snuggle.
I just knew.

Soon, the beating of his drum slowed down. Tony didn't talk to the other kids, but he whispered in my ear, "I don't like school."

My pretty hairdo drooped a little. I wasn't sure I liked school either.

During recess, a girl named Bessie was sad.

I stayed with her and felt little raindrops plop on my head.

"I want to go home," she said.

It was time to snuggle again.

I just knew.

I snuggled in Bessie's arms until the raindrops stopped falling.

After recess, I heard a strange noise!

BUZZ BUZZ BUZZ

I thought it might mean danger. I ran out of the school, pushing the doors open and pulling Dee as hard as I could. All the children followed us, staring at me. It turned out to only be a fire drill. I was embarrassed.

When we returned to the classroom, I wanted to snuggle with them. But they snuggled me first. *They just knew.*

At noon, the school was filled with the smells of food. One boy told a silly story about a dog who ate "people food" and turned into a person. Then the boy barked like a dog.

Everyone laughed at the silly story, even Bessie and Tony.

His barks didn't really sound like a dog, but I still thought it was pretty funny.

Later that afternoon, the teacher said, "Let's learn about numbers." Some of the kids showed their pouty faces. "I don't know how to count," said one. "I don't like numbers," said another. The teacher said, "Dolly has four legs. 1-2-3-4. We have two legs. 1-2. Four is greater than two. That means Dolly has more legs than we do."

The pouty faced kids counted their legs and my legs. Then they turned their pouts upside down.

I didn't know that I had more legs than people! I helped the kids learn!

I stood up straight and my hairdo did, too.

After math, the teacher told the kids to draw the best part of their day. Bessie drew a picture of her and me standing on the green grass with a big yellow sun in the sky. No raindrops.
She's my friend! I was sure about that.

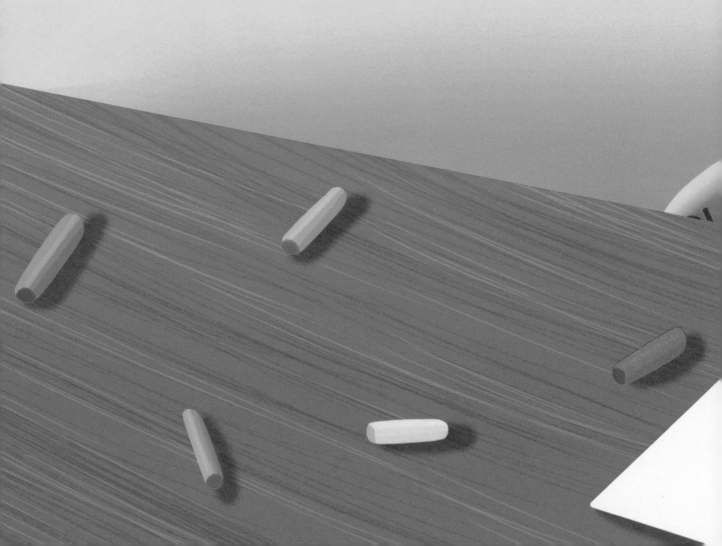

The teacher put all the pictures on the wall. The upside-down pouty faces
drew me, and Tony did too. I looked at the wall of pictures and saw drawings
of me everywhere!

"Do you think Dolly could have one of the pictures?" Dee asked the teacher.

Tony ran to give Dee his picture. YELP! He stepped on my paw.

"I am sorry, Dolly", he said. But I didn't mind.

At three o'clock, the kids said goodbye to each other, the teacher, and even me.

"See ya', Dolly," they said.
Tony shook my paw. Bessie hugged me.

Back at home, Dee removed my pink vest.

"What a day!" she exclaimed.

She was right. What a day!

I had stayed with Bessie on the playground, sat with Tony in reading class, learned about numbers, and helped the other kids learn too.

DOLLY

Dolly

When I first started working, I didn't understand what my job was going to be. I thought I would "come," "sit," and "stay" – and that's all. I suppose any dog can do those things. But my job is to help kids. I closed my eyes and thought about tomorrow.

I was going to do a great job. I was sure about that.

Dee stroked my shaggy head. She had rescued me, loved me,

and helped me do a great job. Now, it was time for us to snuggle.
I just knew.

BEHIND THE STORY

Dolly arrived at her new home with fear and sadness in her eyes.

Dolly's fur was so tangled and messy that **several shampoos were necessary.**

Dolly's yearbook photo clearly shows her love of life.

Dolly and her friend Jenna enjoy a book, **laugh and snuggle.**

The Goff Family.
Top: John, Minnie, Dee, Yogi.
Bottom: Zorro, Dolly and Daisy.

Dolly **'pays it forward'** by helping young children the same way Dee and John helped her – with love. **And snuggles!**

Made in the USA
Columbia, SC
23 April 2024

34549956R00024